D1432576

Before the Beginning Began

Frank Cavalli

illustrated by
Kellee Riley

Star Dome Publishing, LLC

copyright © by Frank Cavalli

illustrations by Kellee Riley

Star Dome Publishing, LLC
PO Box 411300
Melbourne, FL 32941

Star Dome Publishing, LLC

ISBN EAN 10   0 9766662 0 0
ISBN EAN 13 978 0 9766662 0 0
LCCN 2005924135

Printed in Canada

All rights reserved. No part of this book may be reproduced or transmitted in any form or by any means, electronic or mechanical, including photocopying, recording, or any information storage and retrieval system now known or to be invented, without permission in writing from Frank Cavalli, except by a reviewer in connection with a review or inclusion in a magazine, newspaper, or broadcast.

Presented to

_____

From

_____

Date

_____

**For the
children
in your life
and for
the child
within your heart**

We have all tried to answer our children's questions about God. But how do you convey the magnitude and majesty of God and His faithful love for His children? Other than teaching our children a simple prayer, this has been a very difficult task.

Before the Beginning Began is a story that will help you fulfill your children's desire to know more about God and, in the process, answer some questions that you might have had when you were a child.

After the story, there is a section titled *Precious Answers, Precious Thoughts.* You will find over 50 questions about the story to help you explore your child's favorite parts of God's creation and discover what activities they enjoy doing with the many gifts that God has given to them. In this section, you can discuss their responses and have the opportunity to share your answers to the same questions.

Before the Beginning Began provides a rare opportunity for discover, intimacy, and bonding while you share a beautiful story of God in a way that has never been told before.

Before the beginning began
was a long, long,
very long time ago.

Before there was an in to come out of
or an out to come in from...

Before there was a down to go up from
or an up to come down from...

Before there was a left to go right from
or a right to go left from...

Before there were stars above
or an Earth below...

There was nothing ...

Nothing but...

GOD

3 1833 04651 1496

It's difficult to think that once
there was nothing but God.
But it's like when you pray
and you close your eyes.

You see nothing, but God is still there.

Now, you know that
a chicken comes from an egg
and an egg comes from a chicken.
But once upon a time,
there wasn't a chicken to lay an egg
or an egg to give us a chicken.

It was a time when there was nothing
for anything to come from,
except from God.

You might think, "Oh, how boring
for God in all that nothingness,
with no place to go
and nothing to do."

Or maybe you feel sad
because God was all alone
in the dark.

Well, God was not bored
and God was not lonely.
God was happy,
because His heart was filled
with the greatest love there was,
and in His mind, He had
the most wonderful plan for His love…
He would make
the most wonderful creation
in the whole universe…

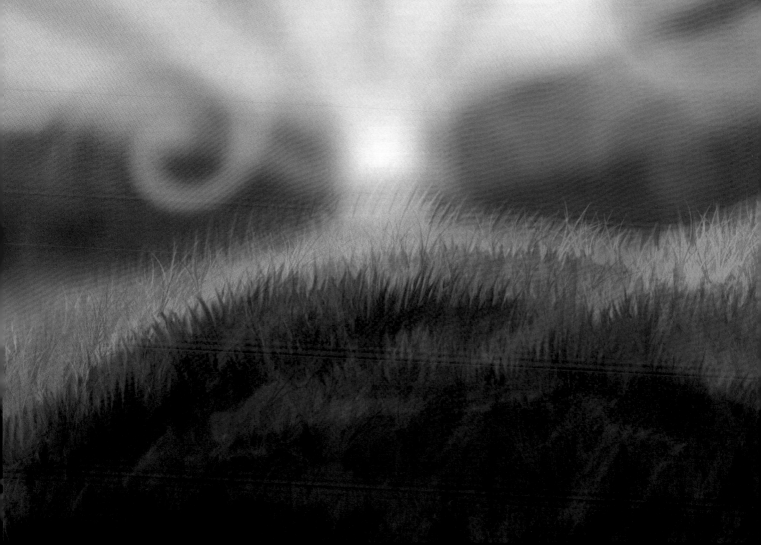

But first, God would create
the most beautiful place
where you and I would live.

So God thought of all
that He could do
and decided
what He would do.

God would create
a warm, golden sun
and a big, blue sky
with fluffy clouds in the day...

and at night,
God would create
a bright moon
and fill the sky
with billions of stars...
some farther than
our eyes could see,
with planets, comets,
and meteors
shooting
across the sky.

God would create
the earth,
where we could
walk and run,
climb and play...

... there would be mountains and valleys, deserts and forests, and jungles, too.

God would create
the gentle rain that would fall
from the clouds in the sky,
so we could see colorful rainbows.

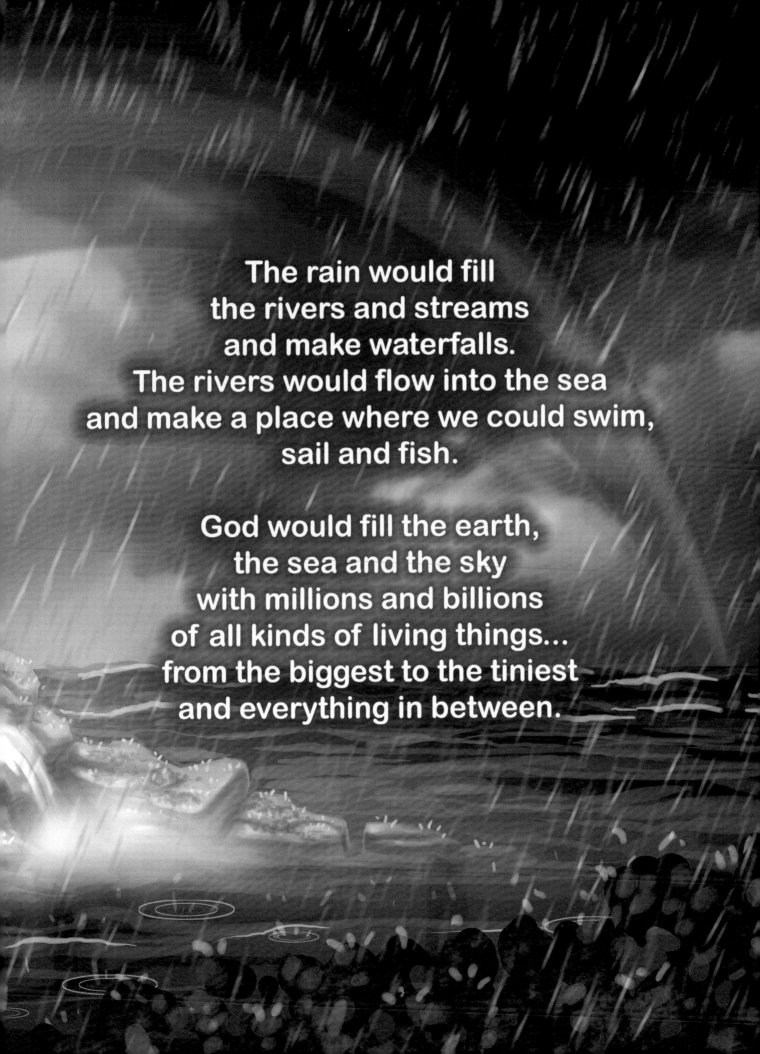

The rain would fill
the rivers and streams
and make waterfalls.
The rivers would flow into the sea
and make a place where we could swim,
sail and fish.

God would fill the earth,
the sea and the sky
with millions and billions
of all kinds of living things...
from the biggest to the tiniest
and everything in between.

God would create
the plants,
from the tallest
redwood tree
to the tiniest blade
of grass.

God would create
the insects,
from the giant beetle
to the tiniest
fairy fly.

God would create
the creatures of the sea,
from the majestic whale
to the tiniest gobi fish.

God would create
the animals,
from the mighty elephant
to the tiniest mouse.

God would create
the birds,
from the magnificent eagle
to the tiniest hummingbird.

God would create
the snakes,
from the enormous anaconda snake
to the tiniest thread snake.

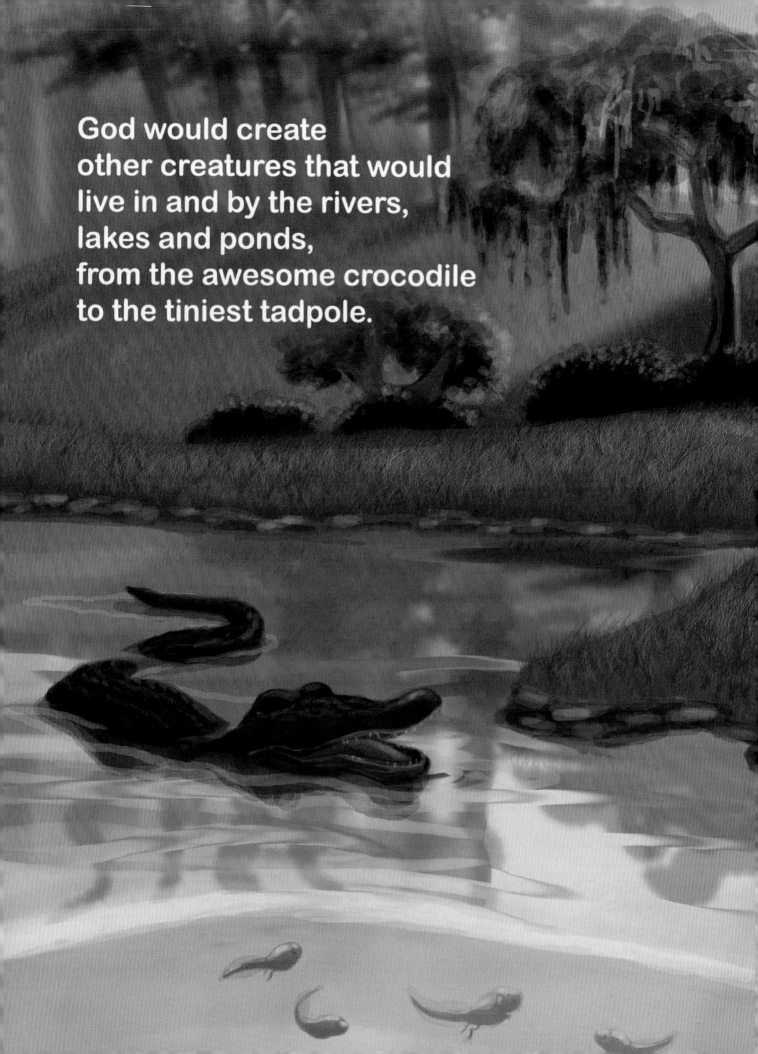

God would create
other creatures that would
live in and by the rivers,
lakes and ponds,
from the awesome crocodile
to the tiniest tadpole.

And finally,
God kept the very best for last...
God would create you and me,
with nothing in between!

God would give us eyes,
so we could see
all the beautiful creations
He had made for us.

God would give us ears,
so we could hear
the lovely sounds
that are all around us.

God would give us a nose,
so we could
smell the different scents
that fill the air.

God would give us a mouth,
so we could taste
the delicious foods
we would eat and drink.

God would give us a voice,
so we could talk, laugh,
sing, and say, "Thank you",
"I'm sorry", and "I love you".

God would give us hands,
so we could touch and feel things,
rough and smooth, soft and hard,
warm and cool.

God would give us arms,
so we could reach out
for what we want
and hug those we love.

God would give us legs and feet,
so we could walk and run
and explore all the different places
He has created for us.

God would give us a mind
so that we could learn about
many things and understand
how much God loves us.

HOLY
BIBLE

God would give us a conscience
so we could be taught
right from wrong
and the good from the bad.

God would give us a will,
so we could do
what God wants us to do
and be what God wants us to be.

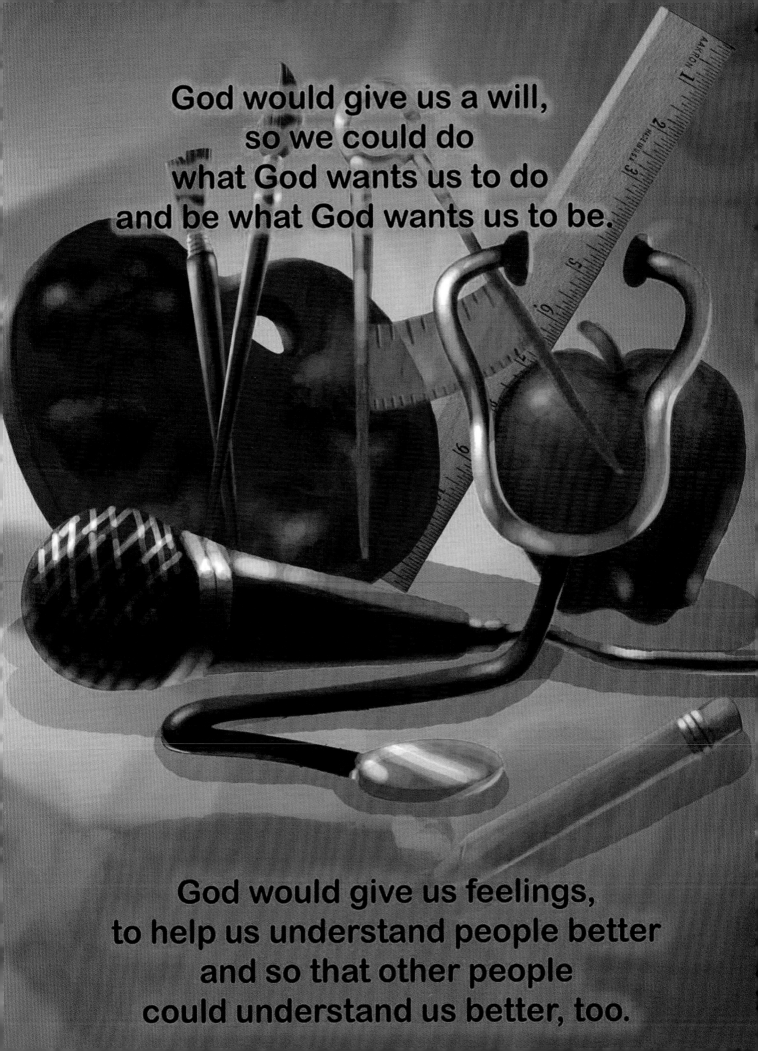

God would give us feelings,
to help us understand people better
and so that other people
could understand us better, too.

God would give us a heart,
so we could love Him,
our family and friends...
even the whole world.

And God would give us a soul
just like He has,
so that someday
we could be with Him
forever in heaven.

Wow! Didn't God make
everything so wonderful!

God thought about what else
could be done. God had an idea.
He would have you and me
take care of all of His creations.
We would keep the air clean
and the water pure.
We would preserve
the mountains and valleys,
the deserts and forests,
and the jungles, too.
We would care for all the creatures
in the air, on the land and in the sea.
We could have whatever we needed
to be happy, as long as
we weren't wasteful and,
most important of all,
we would take care of each other
and be grateful to God for all His gifts.

Then God was ready
to begin the beginning.

Scientists call this moment
"The Big Bang."

While it is true that God can be
loud and powerful
like a big bang,
those words really don't
express His precious love.

So we'll call
the beginning
the moment when
God threw
"The Big Kiss"
into the darkness
and said...

"Let there be..."

LIGHT!

This is not the end...

This is the beginning...

Precious Answers, Precious Thoughts

The following questions will help you explore your child's favorite parts of God's creation and discover what activities they enjoy doing with the many gifts that God has given them. You can discuss their responses and have the opportunity to share with the child your answers to the same questions.

Favorites of our World

God created the plants,
from the tallest redwood tree
to the tiniest blade of grass.

Can you name things that grow?

What is your favorite?

Why?

God created the insects,
from the giant beetle
to the tiniest fairy fly.

Can you name any insects?

What is your favorite?

Why?

God created the creatures
of the sea, from the majestic
whale to the tiniest gobi fish.

Can you name any creatures
that live in the sea?

What is your favorite?

Why?

God created the animals,
from the mighty elephant
to the tiniest mouse.

Can you name any animals?

What is your favorite?

Why?

God created the birds,
from the magnificent eagle
to the tiniest hummingbird.

Can you name any birds?

What is your favorite?

Why?

God created the snakes,
from the enormous
anaconda snake to the
tiniest thread snake.

Can you name any snakes?

What is your favorite?

Why?

God created other creatures that live in and by the rivers, lakes, and ponds, from the awesome crocodile to the tiniest tadpole.

Can you name any creatures that live in and by rivers, lakes, and ponds?

What is your favorite?

Why?

Favorites About You and Me

God gave us eyes, so we could see all the beautiful creations He made for us.

What beautiful things do you like to see?

What is your favorite?

Why?

God gave us ears, so we could hear the lovely sounds that are all around us?

What sounds do you like to listen to?

What is your favorite?

Why?

God gave us a nose, so we could smell the different scents that fill the air.

What scents do you like to smell?

What is your favorite?

Why?

God gave us a mouth,
so we could taste the delicious
food we would eat and drink.

What do you like to eat and drink?

What is your favorite? Why?

God gave us a voice, so we could talk, laugh, sing and say, "Thank you", "I'm sorry", and "I love you".

What things do you like to talk about?

What songs do you like to sing?

What is your favorite song? Why?

God gave us hands, so we could touch and feel different things, rough and smooth, soft and hard, warm and cold.

What things do you like to touch and feel?

What is your favorite?

Why?

God gave us legs and feet, so we could walk and run and explore all the different places He created for us.

What places do you want to explore?

Why?

God gave us a mind, so that we could learn about many things and understand how much God loves us.

What things do you want to learn about?

What is your favorite?

Why?

How do you know God loves you?

God gave us a conscience, so that we could be taught right from wrong and the good from the bad.

What things are good?

What things are not good?

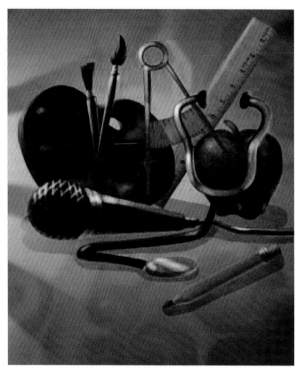 God gave us a will, so that we could choose what God wants us to do and be what God wants us to be.

What do you think
God wants you to do?

What do you think
God wants you to be?

God gave us feelings, to help us understand people better and so that other people could understand us better, too.

How do you know when people are happy?

How do you know when people are sad?

God gave us a heart,
so that we could love Him,
our family and friends...
even the whole world.

How do you show someone
you love them?

How can you love the
whole world?

And God gave us a soul.

If your child's responses to these questions are particularly
precious, interesting, or funny, please E-mail them to

answers@StarDomePublishing.com

Please include the child's name and age. Your submissions will be considered for
posting on our website for the world to read and enjoy! Or you may mail them to

Star Dome Publishing, LLC
PO Box 411300
Melbourne, FL 32941

Order Form

Please send me _____ copies of **Before the Beginning Began** at $19.95 each.

Name _____

Shipping Address _____

City _____

State _____ Zip Code _____

Payment: _____ **check** _____ **credit card**

_____ books at $19.95 each = _____

shipping charges = _____ ($4.00 for first book; $2.00 ea. additional copy)

FL residents add 7% sales tax = _____

Total amount due _____

Credit Card Orders _____ VISA _____ MasterCard

Card Number _____3-digit security code_____

Name on card _____ Exp. Date _____

Signature _____

Telephone Number _____

Mail to:	Star Dome Publishing LLC
	PO Box 411300
	Melbourne, FL 32941
Fax to:	321-757-0396
	Or order from: www.StardomePublishing.com